This book belongs to

The Magic Chest of OZ

THE MAGIC CHEST
OF OZ

Written and Illustrated

By

Donald Abbott

NEW YORK

The Emerald City Press

The Magic Chest of Oz

Printed in the U.S.A.

The Emerald City Press
A Division Of
Books of Wonder®
132 Seventh Avenue
New York, NY 10011

ISBN 0-929605-20-9 (paperback)

2 3 4 5 6 7 8 9

TABLE OF CONTENTS

The Corn and the Crow 1

The Haunted House 12

The Tin Woodman 21

The Hammer-Heads 35

The King of the Forest 41

The Celebration 51

The Shadow 57

The Witch of the North 69

The Imp 75

The Silver Acorn 80

The Black Tower 88

The Rainbow Army 96

The Magic Chest of OZ

The Corn and the Crow

The first annual celebration of Dorothy Day was only a week away and the people of the Land of Oz were busy getting ready. Pictures of the little girl were hung up in every town and village, clever craftsman made cloth dolls of Dorothy and her dog Toto, while wandering musicians travelled the land and sang her praises.

Now for those of you who don't remember – and shame on you if you don't – Dorothy Gale was the little girl from Kansas who was whisked away by cyclone and dropped into Oz. Along with her friends – the Scarecrow, the Tin Woodman and the Cowardly Lion – she had many wonderful adventures, and even managed to rid the land of its two wicked witches. But it had been almost a year since she returned home with the aid of the magical silver Shoes, and a grand holiday had been proclaimed to mark the event.

Nowhere were things more festive than at the Emerald City. Banners bearing Dorothy's picture lined the glittering green walls, the streets were decorated with garlands and tinsel, and the air was filled with laughter.

The Ozites, which was the name of the little people who lived in this marvelous city, were

1

dressed in their finest clothing. The men wore highly polished boots, their jackets were lime green in color, and on their heads they wore green pointed hats. The women wore shoes made of jade, their dresses were of green silk, and lovely green ribbons adorned their hair.

Over their eyes the Ozites wore spectacles that were held on their heads by two gold bands, which were fastened together in the back by a tiny lock. All of the spectacles had green glass lenses.

Long ago the Wizard of Oz had decreed that anyone within the walls of the Emerald City must wear a pair of these spectacles. He told the Ozites that the green glass would protect them from being blinded by the dazzling glare of the Emerald City. However, if the truth be told, this city wasn't completely green; but the little Wizard had discovered that by wearing these specially treated glasses, everything that wasn't green would take on a greenish tint. And even though the Wonderful Wizard had long since departed from the Land of Oz, and the Scarecrow now ruled in his place, the people still carried on the tradition.

Inside the Royal Palace, which is at the very heart of the Emerald City, the Scarecrow sat on an emerald-studded throne, mulling over the day-

The Corn and the Crow

to-day matters of state that occupied most of his time as king.

Of course, he really didn't look much like a king. Instead of regal robes made of silk or satin, he wore an old suit of blue clothes that once belonged to the Munchkin farmer who had created him. The suit had been stuffed with straw, which would often bunch up in the arms and legs, causing him to walk about in an awkward and clumsy manner. His head was nothing more than a small sack upon which eyes, a nose, and a mouth had been neatly painted with blue paint. On his head he preferred to wear an old pointed hat instead of a heavy crown of gold.

In spite of his simple appearance, the Scarecrow was a very clever fellow; for the Wizard of Oz had filled his cloth head with highly superior brains made of bran, mixed with pins and needles. Whenever something went wrong around the Emerald City he was always able to get right to the point of the problem, and resolve it with a sharp answer.

As the Scarecrow was reading over some rather important-looking documents, there came a knock at the throne room door.

"Who's there?" he asked.

The Magic Chest of Oz

"The Royal Army of Oz," came the reply.

"Please enter," said the Scarecrow, as he set the documents aside.

The door opened, and in marched a tall soldier in a handsome green uniform, sporting a long green beard. He halted before the emerald throne and saluted.

"Good news, sire," he said. "The Royal Chef has informed me that the cake for the Dorothy Day celebration is ready, and that his assistants are in the banquet hall putting on the final touches."

"Excellent!" shouted the Scarecrow, leaping to his feet. "I must see it at once," he added, rushing from the room. The Soldier with the Green Whiskers followed close behind him.

A few minutes later they were in the banquet hall staring up at a cake that stood at least twenty feet tall. The cake had been baked in the shape of Dorothy and her dog Toto, and a dozen green-clad chefs were scurrying up and down on ladders as they put on the finishing touches with extra icing.

"It's perfect!" sighed the Scarecrow, his painted smile even broader than usual. "What do you think, Royal Army?"

The Soldier with the Green Whiskers had his head tilted way back so he could see the cake more

5

clearly. It looked just like little Dorothy – with Toto at her feet – and was made of green sponge cake and stood so tall that the icing hair on its head just missed touching the ceiling by inches.

"It's a masterpiece," he replied. "Your guests will be overwhelmed when they see it."

"Speaking of my guests," said the Scarecrow, "you did remember to send out the party invitations?"

"Yes, sire."

"Good! Now I want you to stand guard over the cake. Don't let anyone stick their fingers in the icing."

"It will be safe while I'm on duty," stated the soldier, giving a smart salute.

"I knew I could count on you," said the Scarecrow, confidently. "Now I must check on my corn."

Waving his arms awkwardly about, while walking on the sides of his boots, the Scarecrow left the banquet hall and went to a small field of corn that was growing behind the palace. A look of pride crossed his cloth face as he viewed the field. The stalks grew tall and straight, a wall of leafy green, and the ears of corn that crowned them were plump and golden.

The Corn and the Crow

"I'll serve this fine corn to my guests when they come to celebrate Dorothy Day," the Scarecrow thought to himself.

As he continued to admire his handiwork, a half eaten ear of corn came flying out from behind the stalks and hit him on the head. Being stuffed with straw he wasn't hurt, but he was surprised by the incident. The Scarecrow picked up the half eaten ear in his gloved hand and examined it.

"A poacher!" he exclaimed.

As quietly as possible the Scarecrow made his way to the back of the cornfield, and there he discovered a large black crow pecking at the corn.

"Stop that!" ordered the Scarecrow. "You can't eat my corn."

The crow looked up at him with cold beady eyes. "I'm the King of the Crows," he squawked. "I can do anything that I please." Then the bird went back to pecking.

"But I'm a scarecrow – aren't you afraid?"

"Afraid of you?" chuckled the Crow King. "I've seen more terrifying rag dolls."

The Scarecrow was angered by the crow's rude manner, and he knew he had to find a way to get rid of the greedy bird before he ate up all the corn. Looking about he saw a shovel resting against a fence, and he had an idea how he could chase away the crow.

Grabbing the shovel in his padded hands he lifted it above his head and rushed at the bird. However, the shovel was made of metal, far too heavy for a scarecrow stuffed with straw to hold up for very long, and the great weight caused him to fall down in a heap.

As the Scarecrow struggled to get back on his feet, he could hear the black bird laughing hysterically. "Please stop!" cried out the Crow King, gasping for breath. "I can't take any more."

"Are you ready to leave my cornfield?" asked the Scarecrow, sternly.

"If I don't I'll die laughing," replied the bird, as he flapped his mighty wings and rose up into the air. "Besides, I've eaten enough for today – but I'll be back tomorrow."

Then the Crow King flew over the back wall of the palace and was gone.

The cornfield was in grave danger and the Scarecrow knew he had to find a way to protect it. So he sat down on the fence and began to think.

An hour later the Scarecrow leaped to his feet in excitement. "I have it!" he shouted and rushed off to the workshop of the Royal Glassblower.

The Magic Chest of Oz

When the wicked crow returned the next day he found the Scarecrow standing patiently in front of the cornfield.

"Are you here to stop me from eating your delicious corn?" asked the Crow King, as he circled above the field.

"Not at all," replied the Scarecrow, cheerfully.

"You're not going to try and frighten me?" asked the bird, wearily.

"No."

"You're not going to chase me?"

The Scarecrow stepped to one side and said, "I know when I've met my match – the corn is all yours."

"It would seem that I misjudged you," said the Crow King. "You're not as stupid as you look."

The black bird chuckled with wicked glee as he flew straight for the nearest ear of corn, but before he reached it his beak struck against something hard, and he fell to the ground with a thud.

"Ohhh!" moaned the crow.

"Is something wrong?" inquired the Scarecrow.

The Crow King leaped to his feet, his beady eyes trained on the cornfield. "What's this?" he shrieked. "A huge glass dome is covering the whole field."

The Corn and the Crow

"Yes," said the Scarecrow, smiling. "I forgot to warn you about that. The Royal Glassblower spent all night making this dome out of enchanted glass. Nothing can break it."

"Bah!" squawked the Crow King, angrily. "You may have outsmarted me for now — but I'll get even with you someday."

The black bird launched himself into the air and flew straight for the Scarecrow's head. At the very last moment he turned aside, disappearing over the back wall of the Royal Palace.

Once he was alone, the Scarecrow removed a glass key from his pocket and put it into a keyhole on the glass dome. Magically, a door opened, allowing him access to the cornfield.

"Now maybe I can have a little peace around here," he said, as he entered the dome and began to tend his prized corn.

The Haunted House

Deep in the Great Eastern Forest of Oz, three men made their way down a very overgrown section of the Yellow Brick Road. They were dressed all in blue from the pointed hats on their heads to the shiny boots on their feet, and since blue was the favorite color of the Munchkin people, it was obvious that these men were Munchkins. The elder gentleman who led the group had a long gray beard. The two men behind him wore leather aprons, while one carried a hammer and the other had a saw slung over his shoulder.

"How much farther is it?" groaned the first Munchkin carpenter. "My poor feet are killing me."

"Quiet!" whispered the second Munchkin carpenter. "Boq will hear you."

They trudged on in silence for half a mile more, when suddenly the Yellow Brick Road came to an abrupt end. Beyond the road, huddled among the trees, stood a shadowy edifice.

"Here we are, boys," Boq announced, coming to a halt. "The former home of the Wicked Witch of the East."

The two Munchkin carpenters looked up at the house and shuddered. It was a massive structure

12

of wood and stone that stood deep in a part of the forest where no sunlight ever penetrated. A dark, very unpleasant-looking place, with dirty windows and a half open front door. There were cracks in the stone foundation, the blue paint on the walls had faded, and dead leaves covered the dome-shaped roof.

"What have we gotten ourselves into?" gasped the first carpenter.

"Quiet!" said the second carpenter. "He will hear you."

They glanced over at Boq. The elder Munchkin was a well-respected farmer, and he had asked them to do a small job for him.

"Beven and Peven," said Boq, turning to face the two carpenters. "You both know that when the Wicked Witch was destroyed by Dorothy's house, all the magic spells she had cast by witchcraft began to fade. This house was maintained by witchcraft, and with her gone it quickly fell into ruin."

"It sure did," said Beven, as he nervously adjusted the hammer in his belt.

Peven nodded his head in agreement as he lowered his saw.

"The walls are cracking," continued Boq, "the

floor boards are rotting, and the roof leaks. The house has become a danger to anyone who might enter. So I want you boys to board it up securely."

The carpenters looked at the creepy old place, then at each other. Their knees were knocking together from fright.

Boq stroked his grey beard. "As the senior member of the Munchkin City Council I promised everyone this danger would be rectified, so I'm counting on you both."

"But they say the witch's house is haunted," said Beven.

"My brother is right," added Peven. "Strange sounds come from this part of the forest at night."

"Nonsense!" Boq exclaimed. He was worried that the carpenters were going to run home and not take the job. "There aren't any ghosts around here."

The carpenters shivered visibly at the mention of ghosts.

"It's a one day job at most – and I know you boys would never let me down," said the elder Munchkin.

The two brothers thought for a moment. When they started out as carpenters it was Boq who gave them their first job and got them many others afterwards. When their cow wandered off into the Blue Marsh, it was Boq who helped them find her, and he ruined a good pair of boots doing it. And when their old mother was taken ill last winter, it was Boq who gathered together the best doctors in Munchkinland to tend to her needs until she was better. The carpenters owed a great deal to the kindness of the elder Munchkin, and they knew deep in their hearts that they couldn't refuse his request.

"You can count on my brother and me," stated Beven.

"We're the best carpenters in all the Munchkin Country," proclaimed Peven, proudly.

"Great!" said Boq, grinning. "Now I must return home. I've been invited to celebrate Dorothy Day at the Emerald City, and I must prepare for the journey."

Boq went back down the Yellow Brick Road, and the two carpenters went to work.

"First we have to know how many doors and windows there are," Beven told his brother. "I want you to go and count them."

"Why me?" asked Peven, a quiver of fear in the tone of his voice. He was terrified at the thought of walking around the witch's house alone.

"Because you're so much better with numbers than I am," Beven replied.

"Oh – you're right," sighed Peven, and he set off about the task.

A few minutes later he returned and informed his brother that there were four doors and thirty windows.

"We'll need a lot of boards to cover all that," said Beven, thoughtfully. "You better get your saw and start cutting down some trees..."

"There's a large wooden shed out back," interrupted Peven. "We could take it apart and use that wood."

"Good idea! Let's get to work."

The carpenters quickly took the walls and roof of the shed apart, and while Peven stacked the wood, his brother started pulling up the floor.

Suddenly Beven cried out.

"What's wrong?" shouted Peven, running over to his brother.

"There's a tunnel under this floor," replied the excited carpenter, who was kneeling over a large hole.

The other carpenter looked at the opening just beneath the wooden floor and saw a round hole with a flight of stone steps going down into darkness. "It's probably just a root cellar," said Peven, a cold chill running over his body as he looked at the black hole.

"Don't be stupid," snapped Beven, getting to his feet. "The Wicked Witch of the East stole many wonderful things from the Munchkin people. Gold chains, silver rings, and jeweled crowns. But after her death none of the plundered items were ever found. This tunnel must be the secret entrance to her treasure vault."

Peven gasped. "You don't plan on going down in there?"

"Of course," replied his brother. "If we recover the stolen items, we'll be heroes."

Beven reached into his pocket and pulled out a box of matches. Lighting two matches, he handed one to his brother and said, "I'll lead the way — you just watch your step."

"You're not getting me to go down there," protested Peven. "Who knows what is inside that hole."

"Our people's stolen things!" returned Beven, who was already starting down the steps. "I'm going to need your help to carry the pilfered goods back above ground," he added, sternly. "Now, come on."

Reluctantly, Peven followed his brother down the stone steps.

The tunnel walls were made of damp blocks of black stone, and as the tunnel wound its way deep into the earth, the two carpenters felt like they were inside a giant snake. White cobwebs – the strands of which were thick like cord – filled the inside of the tunnel. The carpenters had to push their way through them with some effort, but after what seemed like an eternity of walking, the steps came to an end.

Before them was a round chamber made of the same black stone as the tunnel, and in the center of the chamber was a large chest. The chest was made of a strange blue metal that seemed to glow, and though the chamber was filled with cobwebs like inside the tunnel, the chest was untouched by them.

"The stolen treasure!" Beven shouted, rushing to the chest.

Examining it he found a small brass key sticking out of the lock. Beven turned the key until he heard the lock click, then he lifted the lid. His face dropped when he looked inside. There wasn't any gold, or silver, or jewels. There wasn't any treasure at all. What he saw inside the chest was a neatly folded blue sheet.

"There isn't any treasure – just a stupid sheet."

"Why would the Wicked Witch of the East go to all this trouble to hide a sheet?" asked Peven, confused.

"How should I know?" snapped Beven, as he kicked the chest. "Maybe she didn't want her guests to steal her best linen."

Something moaned.

"What was that?" gasped Beven.

"I don't know," replied Peven, shaking. "But I think it came from the chest – right after you kicked it."

There was a second moan, and the carpenters watched in horror as a large blue, shapeless form rose up from inside the metal chest. The sheet had come to life, and at the top of the swirling haze were two burning red eyes that were cruelly staring down at them.

"A ghost!" they screamed in unison, rushing for the tunnel steps.

The brothers took the steps two at a time, and when they reached the surface they ran off down the Yellow Brick Road as fast as they could, not stopping until they were safe at home. Both of them vowed never to return to the witch's house again.

Meanwhile, deep in the underground chamber, in the gloom just behind the glowing chest, one of the shadows stirred. Then the eerie silence of the room was broken as the shadow began to laugh.

The Tin Woodman

In the throne room of the Royal Palace of the Winkies, which is in the western part of the Land of Oz, the Tin Woodman was preparing for a journey. He was a most remarkable man, made entirely of tin. His arms and legs and head were skillfully jointed to his body, enabling him to move about with perfect ease. On his chest was a small metal patch, and behind it rested the red silk heart given him by the Wizard of Oz.

The Winkie people became very fond of the Tin Woodman when he visited them during his adventures with Dorothy; and since their former ruler, the Wicked Witch of the West, had been melted by a pail of water, they asked him to rule over them in her stead. The Tin Woodman heartily accepted the offer, and had since governed the little people with kindness.

Recently he had received an invitation from his friend the Scarecrow, asking him to travel to the Emerald City and help host the Dorothy Day celebration. He was highly complimented by this honor, and excited at the thought of seeing his old companion again, so he set about making things ready for the long trip.

Suddenly the double doors of the throne room

burst open and in rushed the Chief Steward of the Winkies. He was a skinny man, dressed in rich yellow robes and carrying a wicker basket in his bony hands.

"Your Majesty," he puffed, trying to catch his breath. "I filled your oil can and placed it in this basket."

"Well done, Chief Steward," said the Tin Woodman. "Now I can start on my journey." He put his metal hand gently on the skinny man's shoulder. "Take good care of the kingdom while I'm gone."

"Have no fear," the steward assured him. "I shall keep everything running smoothly during your absence."

So shouldering his axe, the Tin Woodman set off for the Emerald City. He walked along through the western countryside for a full day and night without stopping, for being made of tin he didn't need to eat or sleep.

As the sun rose on the second day of his journey, a strange melody filled the morning air, and brought the Tin Woodman to a sudden stop. He listened attentively to the music, which was soft and soothing to the ear, yet filled with sadness. Fighting back a tear, he turned aside from his travels and followed after the music.

The melody led him to a small hill, behind which sat a young man with a round face, sharp green eyes and a head of straw-colored hair. His cloak and tunic were bright yellow, trimmed along the edges with gold thread, and on his feet he wore a pair of black boots. In his lap rested a beautiful golden harp, and he plucked on the string with loving care.

"Your music is wonderful," said the Tin Woodman, as he walked around the hill. "But why is it so sad?"

The young man looked up, and seeing the Tin Woodman he leaped to his feet, bowing low. "Your Majesty," he said. "Please forgive me – but my heart is almost broken."

"Hearts are of special interest to me," said the Tin Woodman, placing his hand over the metal patch on his chest. "Tell me what troubles you."

"I am Sir Dashabout the Minstrel," began the young man. "Once I was the happiest man in all the Land of Oz, for the lovely Lady Cynthia had consented to marry me. I spent every day composing songs about her beauty, and my heart was filled with love."

The Tin Woodman sighed.

The Tin Woodman

"But yesterday my happiness came to an end. My beloved and I were taking a noonday stroll, when a wicked imp rushed up and carried Cynthia away."

"This is terrible!" exclaimed the Tin Woodman, outraged. "We must find this imp and force him to release Lady Cynthia at once."

Sir Dashabout hung his head sadly. "His name is Etuous, and he lives in a small grove not far from here. But the trees that surround the grove are enchanted, and won't allow anyone to pass through them."

"Show me to this grove!" commanded the Tin Woodman.

Sir Dashabout led him to a saucer-shaped valley, in the middle of which stood a ring of thirteen trees. The trees were tall and broad, and their leafy branches grew so closely together that the grove beyond them could not be seen. Each of the trees had a face growing in its gnarled bark, and their wooden eyes were trained on the two strangers who were entering the valley.

"Those are the enchanted trees that serve the imp," said the minstrel. "They are very, very dangerous."

"Hmph!" said the Tin Woodman. "I was a

The Magic Chest of Oz

Woodman before I was the Ruler of the Winkies, and I know a thing or two about trees."

Still they approached the grove with caution.

The largest of the thirteen trees, who was their leader, began to frown. "Go away!" he demanded, as he shook his branches violently. "You are not welcome here."

"That's not very polite," said the Tin Woodman.

The Leader of the Trees was taken back. "What do you want here, tin man?"

"I want to enter your grove."

"People are not allowed inside the grove," barked the Leader.

"Why not?"

"Imp Etuous has ordered it so," was the gruff answer.

"And why do you serve this wicked imp?" inquired the Tin Woodman.

The Leader of the Trees groaned. "We have no choice. He possesses the Silver Acorn – a magic charm that compels us to obey him."

"Woe is me," cried Sir Dashabout. "The Lady Cynthia is a prisoner forever."

The Tin Woodman handed his basket to the minstrel and lowered the axe from his shoulder. "Well I'm afraid that I must enter the grove – with

26

or without your permission," he said, rubbing his tin jaw. "A young woman is in danger."

"Then we must stop you," snapped the Leader, frowning so hard that some of the bark above his brow began to crack.

Determined, the Tin Woodman started for an opening between two of the trees, but their branches blocked his way. With one quick movement the woodman took his axe in both hands and swung it with all his might, chopping off two of the lower branches.

All the trees began to shudder violently.

"Stop!" shouted the Leader of the Trees, his face drawn with pain.

"Will you let me pass?" asked the Tin Woodman, his axe poised for a second strike.

"Let him pass! Let him pass!" pleaded the twelve trees.

"Very well," moaned the Leader. "Imp Etuous told us to keep out people – he didn't say anything about nasty tin creatures. Enter and leave us in peace."

"You wait here," the Tin Woodman told Sir Dashabout. "I will soon return with Lady Cynthia." Then he passed between the trees. The grove wasn't very big, and in its center grew a

giant white mushroom. Sitting on the mushroom was a young woman wearing a pale yellow dress. Her face was delicate; like a fine china doll, her eyes were deep sea blue, and her hair was long and golden.

Next to her stood an ugly little man about three feet tall, clutching a wooden club twice his size. He had big round eyes, a pointed nose and a wicked grin. His clothing was dark brown, and fit tightly over his small frame, while pinned to his collar was a charm in the shape of a silver acorn.

"Please let me go," Lady Cynthia begged the imp.

"Impossible!" said Imp Etuous. "You are my prisoner – just as I am a prisoner of your beauty."

Lady Cynthia took out a lace handkerchief and began to cry.

"Cry all you want," said the imp. "But you will never leave here."

At that moment the Tin Woodman entered the grove and walked up to the mushroom.

Seeing this metal intruder in his grove, the imp's eyes narrowed with anger. "How dare you enter here?" he shrieked, shaking his giant club. "Prepare to meet your end."

"Hold you temper," demanded the Tin Woodman. "I seek the release of the Lady Cynthia who you have so cruelly kidnapped."

"Never!" exploded Etuous, rushing madly at the Tin Woodman and waving the giant club over his head.

"I was hoping to solve this without any violence," sighed the Tin Woodman, as he gripped the handle of his axe tightly. "But you leave me no choice."

Imp Etuous grinned as he thrust his club forward. "Your doom is upon you, intruder."

Without hesitating, the woodman swung his axe, chopping the giant club in half. Surprised, the imp stared at his severed weapon.

"Look what you have done!" howled Etuous. "That was a perfectly good club – and now it's ruined."

"Now will you end this foolishness and release your captive?" asked the Tin Woodman, lowering his axe.

Gritting his teeth, and waving his fists wildly, the imp rushed at the Tin Woodman. There was a terrible crash when he struck his head on the woodman's metal chest, and the little creature fell to the ground unconscious.

"Hoo-ray!" shouted Lady Cynthia, leaping to her

feet. "You have saved me."

"It would appear so," replied the Tin Woodman, surprised by this strange turn of events. "Now we had better leave before the imp wakes up."

The Tin Woodman took one last look at the motionless imp, and he noticed the Silver Acorn pinned to his collar. He remembered what the Leader of the Trees had told him about the imp possessing a magic charm that controlled trees, and this gave him an idea. He removed the Silver Acorn from the little man's collar, then he led Lady Cynthia out of the grove.

"You're a most remarkable creature," said the Leader of the Trees, as he watched the Tin Woodman emerge from the grove. "It's not an easy task to overpower an imp – especially one as wicked as Etuous."

The Tin Woodman walked over to the Leader, and holding up the Silver Acorn he asked, "Is this the charm that he used to control you and the other trees?"

"That's it," said the Leader, disgust in his eyes as he looked upon the magic charm. "All the trees in Oz must obey whoever bears it."

"Then you will do anything that I ask of you?"

said the Tin Woodman.

The Leader looked at him grimly. "What do you wish of us?"

"Just that you and the other trees keep the imp a prisoner inside the grove so he can't cause anymore trouble."

"An excellent idea!" roared the Leader, his wooden features beaming with delight. "It shall be done."

The Tin Woodman placed the Silver Acorn under his cap for safe keeping; then he turned to tell Sir Dashabout and Lady Cynthia that the wicked imp would never bother them again, only to find the two sweethearts locked in a tender embrace. The sight touched him deeply, and tears of joy streamed down his metal cheeks.

"How can we ever thank you enough?" asked Sir Dashabout, smiling from ear to ear.

The Tin Woodman went to reply, but found that the tears had rusted his jaw shut. Frantically he pointed to the wicker basket, which the minstrel quickly handed back to him. Removing the oil can from inside the basket he carefully oiled the hinges of his mouth, and soon it began to move.

"Ah – that's much better," he said, returning the oil can to the basket. Then he looked at the happy couple and said, "Seeing you together is all the thanks I need."

Lady Cynthia walked up to the Tin Woodman and kissed him on the forehead. "You have a good heart, sir."

"I like to think so," he replied, with a bashful smile. "Now I must be on my way. There's an old friend waiting for me."

This said, the Tin Woodman shouldered his axe, waved good-bye, and continued on his way.

The Hammer-Heads

Far to the south of the Emerald City, in the great Quadling wilderness, stands a high hill covered with crooked rocks. Among these rocks live the Hammer-Heads; a most disagreeable group of people with stout round bodies and flat heads. They have no arms or hands. Instead their large heads sit atop very wrinkled necks, and with a single thought they can cause their necks to stretch out to a great length, projecting their heads forward like living jack-in-the-boxes.

Under the high hill, accessible only through a well-guarded tunnel, was a large damp cavern. The cavern was lit by a pale white glow that came from a giant diamond lodged in the vaulted roof, and sitting beneath the diamond was an extremely fat Hammer-Head. He had brilliant orange hair, a round nose and big feet. This was King Blugo the Bold, supreme ruler of the Hammer-Heads, and a very unpleasant fellow.

Every day Blugo would sit upon his uncomfortable throne of rocks and think nasty thoughts. He hated all the good people of Oz, because they lived in cozy houses and ate fine foods, while he lived among the cold rocks and ate only roots.

"What I wouldn't give for a nice soft bed and a

slice of chocolate cake," he would often think to himself. "But all I ever get is a dirt floor and smelly old roots."

Today Blugo was in an especially foul mood. The roots he ate for breakfast that morning had been sour, and now he had terrible stomach pains.

"Roots, roots and more roots," he moaned. "My poor tummy hurts because of those wicked things." He paused to let out a groan. "Just once I'd like to wake up and find a nice piece of chocolate cake waiting for me. Oh – the pain!"

From the shadowy darkness of the tunnel a harsh voice called out his name.

"King Blugo the Bold!"

The king jumped up, his neck extending out a few feet, while his flat head hovered before the dark opening. "Who is there?" he demanded.

"A friend," came the reply.

This made Blugo very suspicious – since he didn't have any friends. "Who are you really?" he asked, gruffly. "And how did you get past my guards?"

Two red eyes glowed from inside the tunnel. "I'm a very powerful friend," answered the voice, "and I have come to you with an offer."

"What kind of offer?" questioned the king. "But

be warned – if the offer isn't to my liking I will call for my guards, and no amount of darkness will conceal you from my rage."

A shrill laugh rose from the tunnel and echoed through the cavern like thunder.

"Join forces with me," said the voice, once the laughter had faded, "and I shall see that you and your people are given the same luxuries that the other inhabitants of Oz possess."

"Tell me more," said King Blugo, interested.

"Help me to conquer the Emerald City and you won't have to live in this damp cavern any longer. Instead you'll have a fine house, comfortable furniture, and rich food."

The mere thought of possessing all these things made King Blugo's head spin, and he completely forgot about his stomach-ache. Still, when his head finally cleared he began to wonder if this unseen 'friend' could really deliver what was promised.

"Show yourself!" demanded the king, his head returning to his body. "I refuse to deal with people who lurk in the shadows like a thief."

"If you insist," said a clown, stepping out from the dark tunnel.

The clown wore a white, cone-shaped hat, a baggy white suit, white gloves and floppy white

shoes. However, the most unusual thing about the clown was the face, which was a rubber mask that completely covered his head.

"What nonsense is this?" Blugo shouted, angrily. "If this is a joke..."

"This isn't a joke," said the clown, cutting off the king in mid-sentence. "Now will you help me invade the Emerald City?"

"Impossible!" roared the King of the Hammer-Heads. "The Emerald City is ruled by the Scarecrow, and he is a friend of the Good Witches of Oz. If we were to attack him the witches would surely come to his aid. And what can a clown do against witches?"

The clown gestured with gloved hands, forming invisible symbols in the air, and a large chocolate cake magically appeared at the king's feet.

Blugo's eyes bulged out of his flat head as he looked at this tasty treat. "My Hammer-Heads are at your service," he said, licking his lips.

The clown smiled.

The King of the Forest

The Hungry Tiger stepped out of the forest and moved stealthily towards the river. He was a mighty beast, about the size of a pony, and his tawny fur was covered with black stripes. He had been hungry all morning, which wasn't unusual for this particular cat, but since he couldn't find a meal to suit his tremendous appetite, he decided to go down to the river for a drink.

A meadow of green clover stretched out before the tiger, and beyond the meadow was the river – or at least where it should have been. As the giant feline reached the banks of the river he could hardly believe the sight that met his sharp yellow eyes. The water was gone. The swift flowing river had mysteriously dried up, leaving only a muddy canal to show where it had once been.

Looking around the Hungry Tiger saw that other animals lined the empty river, all searching for water to quench their thirsts.

"What has happened here?" he called out to them.

"We don't know," replied a brown bear, as he scratched his fuzzy head. "One minute we were drinking from the river, and the next minute all the water was gone."

41

"This is terrible!" said the Hungry Tiger. "I must inform the king at once."

With mighty strides the tiger rushed back into the forest, leaping over fallen trees, springing across wide ditches, not stopping until he reached a large clearing. Here sat a huge lion casually licking the sharp claws on his right paw. He was a magnificent animal, at least a head taller than the tiger. Strong muscles rippled beneath the tan fur of his body, and around his head was a thick mane of shaggy golden hair.

This was the former Cowardly Lion, and as the third companion of little Dorothy he had been invited by the Scarecrow to come to the Emerald City and join in on the Dorothy Day celebration. The Lion was just tidying up before starting on his journey, and he was very surprised by the sudden appearance of the Hungry Tiger.

"Have you come to see me off?" asked the Lion.

The Hungry Tiger fell down on all fours. "Oh, King of the Forest, " he panted. "Calamity has befallen us."

"Rise, my friend, and tell me what has upset you so."

The Hungry Tiger told of his trip to the river and what he found there.

"This is a serious matter," said the Lion, gravely. "I must postpone my journey to the Emerald City until after this crisis is resolved."

With a shake of his shaggy mane the Lion rose and headed for the river, the Hungry Tiger following close on his tail. When they arrived at the river they found even more animals gathered, all of them seeking their daily drink of water, all of them faced with disappointment.

"The king is here," chattered a chimpanzee, who was the first to spot the Lion. "He'll bring back the water."

All the animals cheered as the Lion approached the edge of the river bank. There he paused, his keen eyes fixed on the empty river bed below. He lowered his shaggy head and examined the mud carefully.

"There is nothing more I can learn here," he stated, his noble brow wrinkled into a frown. "I must travel up river to discover the cause of this sudden drought."

The Lion travelled north. He moved swiftly along the banks of the river, searching for a clue that might explain what had happened to all the water. The Hungry Tiger and all the other animals raced right behind him.

The King of the Forest

Two hours elapsed without the Lion discovering any answer to the mystery. The Lion feared that magic might be involved in the sudden disappearance, so he sniffed at the air, but couldn't smell the particular odor that magic produced when it was in operation.

Now the animals were travelling through the deepest part of the forest. Here the trees grew tall and close together, their leafy roof allowing only thin shafts of light to filter down. The ground was covered with a tangle of thick foliage, and the animals were forced to slow their pace to a careful walk.

Up ahead the empty river bed took a sharp turn into a wall of overgrown bushes. A clear sense of danger filled the air, and the Lion ordered the animals to hold their ground.

"I shall go on alone from here," he announced.

"Let me accompany you," pleaded the Hungry Tiger. "I feel something evil is lurking just ahead."

"I feel it too, old friend. But I need you to remain here and keep the others calm while I'm gone."

Cautiously, the Lion rounded the gloomy bend, and there, spread from one bank of the river to the other was a large dam made of mud and branches.

A dozen brown beavers were scurrying around the dam, each one hard at work making it stronger.

The Lion let out a mighty roar, causing the beavers to turn, their eyes wide with terror. "What is going on here?" he growled. "By building this dam you have shut off the river from the rest of the forest and deprived your fellow animals." He shook his shaggy head angrily. "You should all know better."

The beavers were all trembling as they bowed low before the Lion. "Please forgive us," they cried out. "We were forced to build it."

"Who would force you to do a wicked thing like this?"

"They serve me," answered a deep voice.

A gray wolf emerged from the forest on the opposite side of the river. He was a giant beast, clearly as large as the Lion himself. He paused at the edge of the river bank, sitting upright on his hind legs, his cold blue eyes fixed on the King of the Forest.

"Who are you?" asked the Lion.

The Wolf smiled, his long snout opening wide to reveal two rows of sharp white teeth. "I am the Great Gray Wolf," he replied with a snarl, "and this river now belongs to me."

The King of the Forest

Then the great beast strolled out onto the dam. "If the animals of this forest want a drink they must come to me. I'll be happy to let them have a drink – for a price."

"And what do you intend to charge them for this privilege?" asked the Lion.

"They must proclaim me their new King of the Forest," replied the Wolf. "It's a small thing to ask," he added with a sneer, "if they don't want to die of thirst."

"Villain!" snapped the Lion, anger raging in his green eyes. "You can't steal the title – it must be earned."

Suddenly, the Hungry Tiger leaped out from behind some bushes and landed beside the Lion. "We will never call you king," he shouted at the wolf.

All the other animals crowded in behind him. "We have only one king!" they cried out. "We want no other!"

"I'm sorry," said the Hungry Tiger, looking over at the Lion. "But we couldn't stay behind."

The lion smiled, pleased by the loyalty demonstrated towards him by his fellow animals. "You have nothing to apologize for."

Lowering his large head, the Great Gray Wolf

stared angrily at the assemblage. "How really touching," he growled through clenched teeth. "But you will bow down to me as your king or you won't drink from my river. It's as simple as that."

"Never!" exclaimed the animals.

"Enough!" said the Lion. "It's time to put an end to this foolishness."

The Lion opened his mouth and began to roar, and the animals covered their ears to protect them from the terrible sound. From his seat on top of the earthen dam the Wolf only grinned with amusement. The roar grew louder, and the ground started to tremble. The grin faded from the Wolf's face, and his pointed ears began to twitch nervously. Straining, the Lion increased the pitch of his roar, and suddenly, the mud and branches that made up the dam gave way.

As the water came cascading forward a chilling howl rose up from the Great Gray Wolf, but it was cut short as the swiftly-moving current crashed down on him. His gray form bobbed about helplessly in the raging river as he desperately sought an escape, but the torrent was far too strong and the Wolf sank beneath the water. He did not resurface.

"It's over," said the Lion, relieved. "Let's all go

49

home."

"But what about your trip to the Emerald City?" asked the Hungry Tiger.

The Lion looked up at the darkening sky. "The sun will be setting soon," he replied. "I'll have to start my journey in the morning and hope the Scarecrow doesn't mind that I arrive a little late."

And so the animals of the forest went to bed that night, secure in the knowledge that the river was flowing once again.

The Celebration

The Emerald City glittered so brilliantly under the bright noonday sun that the Tin Woodman had to shield his eyes against the dazzling glare as he walked up to the emerald-studded gate. Next to the gate was an illuminated green button marked BELL, which he pressed, and from somewhere within the high walls of the city a silvery tone sounded. A moment later the gate was opened by a little man dressed all in green.

"A grand welcome to you, sir," said the Guardian of the Gates. "It's wonderful to see you once again."

"The pleasure is all mine," replied the Tin Woodman. "The Emerald City and its people have always held a warm spot in my heart."

The Guardian gestured to a high arched room just beyond the gate and said, "Please come in. I'll fit you with a pair of spectacles, then personally escort you to the Royal Palace."

The Tin Woodman entered the room and the gate closed behind him. Once inside the Guardian of the Gates opened a big box filled with hundreds of green spectacles. He rummaged through the box until he found a pair that would fit comfortably over the Tin Woodman's eyes, then he led the way out onto the cobblestone streets of the Emerald City.

The Scarecrow was impatiently pacing back and forth in front of the Royal Palace when he saw the Guardian of the Gates and the Tin Woodman approaching. Happily, he rushed forward and clasped his old comrade's metal hand in his own gloved one.

"Hail to the Tin Woodman of Oz," he said, warmly.

"Well met by the Scarecrow of Oz," replied the Woodman.

The two friends embraced.

"If you don't require anything further, sire," said the Guardian, with a bow, "I'll return to my post."

"By all means," replied the Scarecrow. "You have served me well, and I'll see that a large piece of celebration cake is sent out to you later."

Then he turned to the Tin Woodman. "We must hurry inside. The other guests are waiting for us in the banquet hall."

"Is the Lion here?" asked the Woodman, as he rushed after his friend.

"Not yet," was the reply. "A sparrow arrived this morning with a message saying he would be late."

"What about the Good Witches of Oz?"

They started up a flight of marble steps as the Scarecrow answered, "Glinda the Good sent her regrets at not being able to attend. It seems she is in the middle of an important magical experiment, and if she doesn't keep an eye on it for the next few days it might explode."

The Tin Woodman winced. "Magic sure is a tricky business."

"I haven't heard a word from the Good Witch of the North," the Scarecrow added, as he pushed open the doors of the Royal Banquet Hall.

A long table was spread at the center of the hall, directly in front of the giant cake baked in the image of Dorothy Gale. Around the table sat many of the most important inhabitants of Oz. The Mayor of the Munchkins, the Mayor of the Winkies, the Mayor of the Quadlings and the Mayor of the Gillikins were all present. The King of the Winged Monkeys was in attendance, and next to him sat the Queen of the Field Mice. The sorceress Gayelette and her husband Quelala were there, and so was Boq the Munchkin. All the guests were having a merry time as they sipped from goblets cut out of solid emeralds.

The Scarecrow and the Tin Woodman took their seats at the head of the table and the celebration feast began. Green-clad waiters brought in tray after tray of delicious foods which they served to the hungry guests.

"Try the corn," the Scarecrow advised. "I grew it myself."

Just then a curtain drew back, and a clown dressed all in white stepped forward. The clown was pulling a wagon, and on the wagon was a large gold box.

"I don't remember hiring a clown to entertain," the Scarecrow mused to himself.

Leaving the wagon behind, the clown walked up to the banquet table. Waving gloved hands about in the air he produced two green roses, handing one each to the Scarecrow and the Tin Woodman.

"Amazing!" said the Woodman, sniffing at the flower. "The scent is magnificent."

The Scarecrow eyed the clown carefully. Even wearing his green spectacles the clown's clothing appeared white, instead of a light green, and this made him suspicious. "I don't know you, sir. Who asked you to perform here today?"

The clown smiled broadly. "They call me Jolly Jewel, a humble harlequin by trade. I wander the

Land of Oz bringing smiles to all I meet. When I heard of this grand celebration I couldn't stay away."

Jolly Jewel pointed to the gold box. "If you will allow me to continue, I promise you a show that will knock you off your throne." The clown smiled even wider and added, "Figuratively speaking that is."

"This fellow's heart seems to be in the right place," the Tin Woodman whispered to the Scarecrow.

"Very well," said the Scarecrow. "You have my permission to perform."

With a graceful bow the clown rushed to the gold box and threw open the lid. Out popped King Blugo the Bold, a wild look on his face. He was quickly followed by one Hammer-Head soldier after another.

"Oh my!" exclaimed the Tin Woodman.

"Oh no!" shouted the Scarecrow.

The clown began to laugh.

The Shadow

A Hammer-Head is a very strange creature to be sure. At first glance they might seem harmless in appearance, since they haven't any arms on their short, stout bodies, but they really are very dangerous. Their flat heads are hard as rock, and they can thrust them forward on expandable necks. Anyone unfortunate enough to be hit by one of these living projectiles would be facing serious injury. So it isn't hard to imagine the look of terror on the faces of the guests when they saw the Hammer-Head soldiers come popping out of the large gold box.

"We're being invaded!" cried the Mayor of the Munchkins.

"Monsters are loose in the Emerald City!" yelled the Mayor of the Quadlings.

"We shall all be slaughtered!" screamed the Mayor of the Gillikins.

"I'm frightened!" whimpered the Mayor of the Winkies, hiding his face behind a napkin.

"Stay calm everyone!" shouted the Scarecrow, as he waved his arms about frantically. "There is no reason to panic."

The guests remained anything but calm; instead they bolted over the banquet table and headed for the nearest exits. The four mayors managed to avoid the Hammer-Heads long enough to escape through the main doors. Gayelette and Quelala, along with Boq the Munchkin, snuck out through a rear pantry, while the King of the Winged Monkeys flew out an open window with the Queen of the Field Mice on his back.

"This is terrible," said the Tin Woodman, who was shaking so badly he rattled.

"I must do something!" exclaimed the bewildered Scarecrow. "As the King of the Emerald City it is my duty to defend it."

"But I don't see how you can," observed the Woodman. "The Hammer-Heads outnumber us one hundred to one, and more are popping out of that box every minute. We must flee," he urged, "while we still can."

Seeing wisdom in his friend's words the Scarecrow agreed. Both of them headed on tip-toe towards the main door, but halfway there the Scarecrow tripped over the leg of an upturned chair, and as the Tin Woodman helped him back to his feet they were surrounded by Hammer-Head soldiers.

"What shall we do now?" asked the Scarecrow, in distress.

59

"I don't know," replied the Tin Woodman, sadly.

Now King Blugo the Bold had an army numbering eight hundred and eighty soldiers – all of them with a savage disposition – and he watched with extreme pleasure as each one came leaping over the side of the gold box.

Jolly Jewel walked over to the King of the Hammer-Heads and asked, "What do you think of my little invasion so far?"

"I must admit that I was a little apprehensive about your plan at first," he confided to the clown. "When you told me about this magic box, which was bigger on the inside than it is on the outside, and that you could fit my whole army in to it, I almost threw you out of my cavern. But everything is falling into place just like you predicted, and soon I'll have all the chocolate cake I can eat."

Hearing this, the clown began to laugh hysterically.

Then King Blugo turned a cruel eye upon the Scarecrow and the Tin Woodman. "Those two are of no further use. Shall I have them destroyed?"

"Wait!" said Jolly Jewel. "Don't hurt them – at least not yet."

"Oh, you won't let me have any fun," moaned

The Shadow

Blugo.

"Enough of that!" snapped the clown. "Now go and attend to your army."

Blugo stomped away muttering to himself.

"You're no ordinary clown!" shouted the Scarecrow, from his prison inside the ring of Hammer-Head soldiers. "Who are you?"

"Quite true," said Jolly Jewel thoughtfully. "The time for pretense has passed."

Quickly the clown removed the white suit and rubber mask, revealing a dark blue shadow beneath. Now a shadow will usually be found attaching itself to objects, like a living person, and it would only move when the person did, mimicking each action in silhouette. But this shadow had a life of its own. Independent of any other living being, it moved about the room with total ease.

Most frightening of all was the shape the shadow assumed – that of a bony old witch with a hunched back. The witch was dressed all in blue, her skin was blue and wrinkled, her straggly hair was just as blue, but her eyes were like two burning coals that glowed from within this living shade.

"That feels much better," said the Shadow,

stretching. "It's cramped inside that costume."

"She looks just like the Wicked Witch of the East!" gasped the Tin Woodman.

At hearing this remark the Shadow's eyes flared bright red. "I'm not the Witch of the East," she hissed, scornfully. "That witch is quite dead — thanks to Dorothy and her flying house."

"Then who are you?" demanded the Scarecrow.

"I'm her shadow."

A terrible silence descended over the banquet hall as the Scarecrow and the Tin Woodman looked on in amazement at the dark shape before them. Their first instinct was to turn and run away, but the ring of Hammer-Heads that encircled them made that quite impossible.

Finally the Scarecrow broke the silence. "The old Witch of the East is dead and turned to dust, so how can her shadow be alive and well?"

"Aha!" rose the harsh voice of the Shadow.

So hideous and unexpected was the sound that it caused the Scarecrow to lose his balance, and the Tin Woodman had his hands full trying to keep his stuffed friend on his feet.

The Shadow of the Witch gestured to the Hammer-Heads to move away from the captives, then she drew closer, fixing them with her glowing eyes. "I am Malvonia," said the Shadow, her voice dropping down to a whisper, "and I am every bit as powerful as the Witch of the East – maybe even more so." The Shadow glanced around the room, smiling darkly. "Often she dreamed of making this city her own, but it will be me who succeeds where she failed."

The Scarecrow pointed a gloved finger at the Wicked Shadow and said, "You, madam, are an usurper."

Malvonia looked at his cloth face, examining the painted features, and then she started to laugh. "I am the ruler here now, and you are nothing but an overstuffed bag of hay."

"The Scarecrow is the rightful ruler of the Emerald City," protested the Tin Woodman. "None of the Ozites will accept you as long as he's alive."

The Shadow stopped laughing, her mouth twisting into a sneer. "What you say is true, Tin Man. So I'll just have to remedy that."

Malvonia snapped her blue fingers and a match appeared between them. She blew on the match three times and it burst into flame.

"Oh no!" shouted the Scarecrow, his stuffed body trembling as he looked at the one thing capable of destroying him. "Keep that match away

from me."

Slowly the Shadow of the Witch moved towards him. "What's the matter, Scarecrow. Not afraid of a little fire, are you?"

Seeing the danger his friend was in, the Tin Woodman readied his axe and rushed at Malvonia. But the Shadow mumbled some magic words, and the Woodman found that he couldn't move, as if all his metal joints had rusted solid.

"Now it's just you and me," cackled Malvonia, holding the lit match only inches from the Scarecrow's cloth face.

Suddenly, the doors of the banquet hall were thrown open, and in rushed the Soldier with the Green Whiskers, his trusty rifle pointed at the Shadow. She was so surprised by his abrupt appearance that she dropped the match, and the flame winked out. At the same moment her spell over the Tin Woodman faded, and he was free to move once more.

"Release the king at once!" demanded the Royal Army of Oz.

"Attack him, you fools!" Malvonia screamed at the Hammer-Heads. "Finish him off and be quick about it!"

Making faces, and howling fiercely, the Hammer-Heads rushed at the Royal Army of Oz. The soldier pointed his rifle slightly above their flat heads and fired. The loud bang that issued from the gun so terrified the Hammer-Heads that they fell to their knees, all of them whimpering pitifully.

Only King Blugo remained standing, and he was irate at seeing his army in this sorry state. Quick as lightning, his head shot forward on his spring-like neck, hitting the Royal Army square on the chin. Dazed by this vicious attack the Soldier with the Green Whiskers staggered across the room, where he fell unconscious into the giant celebration cake.

With the situation under control, Malvonia turned her attention back to the captives. "Now where was I?" she asked, rubbing her pointed blue chin.

"This looks like the end," sighed the Scarecrow.

"Good-bye, old friend," said the Tin Woodman.

Unexpectedly the banquet hall was enveloped by a blinding flash of light, and when the light had finally dissipated, the Scarecrow and the Tin Woodman had vanished.

The Witch of the North

Sunshine filtered down through cuts in the gray overcast sky, dotting the countryside with patches of warmth. The Scarecrow blinked and the Tin Woodman gasped. They were no longer inside the Royal Banquet Hall. Both of them were now standing on the Yellow Brick Road just outside the high walls of the Emerald City.

"How did we get here?" asked the Tin Woodman, surprised.

"I think the answer is coming now," said the Scarecrow, pointing towards the north.

A spectrum of radiant colors filled the sky, and the two friends watched in awe as the end of a beautiful rainbow settled down on the Yellow Brick Road directly before them. Out of the rainbow stepped a little woman with white hair and a friendly smile. She wore a white pointed hat, and around the wide brim were silver bells that jingled merrily at the slightest movement of her head. Her gown was white, like a puffy cloud on a bright summer's day, and it was dotted here and there with shiny diamonds cut in the shape of stars.

"The Good Witch of the North!" exclaimed the Tin Woodman. "Was it you who rescued us?"

"Yes," she replied, a merry twinkle in her eyes.

"I cast the spell that carried you here. Also, I removed your green spectacles during the transfer. You won't need them now."

"We're safe," said the Scarecrow, "but what about the Emerald City?"

The Good Witch shook her head sadly. "I'm afraid the Hammer-Heads have overrun the city by now, and the Ozites are their prisoners."

"This is terrible," sighed the Scarecrow. "I feel so helpless."

"You are far from helpless," said the little woman, reassuringly. "And you have plenty of friends who will help you as well. In fact, here comes one such friend now."

Sure enough, down the Yellow Brick Road trod the Lion. "What's all this?" he asked. "Did you decide to move the party outdoors?"

The Scarecrow quickly told the great cat what had so recently transpired inside the Emerald City.

"Can't anything be done?" the Lion asked of the Good Witch.

"Maybe," she replied, pensively. "The Hammer-Heads are fierce fighters, but they could never have planned and executed this invasion alone. They rely completely on this Wicked Shadow. So if you could take her captive they would surely surrender."

"But how can we do this?" asked the Tin Woodman.

"It will not be an easy task to capture the Shadow," she advised them, a grave look on her usually pleasant face. "But there is a way."

"Please tell us," pleaded the Scarecrow.

The Good Witch of the North called them all together in a circle. "Listen closely and I will tell you about the day that the Wicked Witch of the East was preparing a particularly nasty potion, and how she accidently spilt some of it on her own shadow. The potion turned her shadow blue, but more importantly, the potion brought her shadow to life. At first the Wicked Witch was amused by this strange turn of events, but when she discovered that the Shadow had been secretly studying her books of witchcraft while she was asleep, the old Witch began to worry. And then the Shadow cast its first spell, and she was truly frightened."

"You mean the Wicked Witch of the East was afraid of her own shadow?" asked the Tin Woodman.

"You could say that," continued the little woman. "But the Witch of the East was very clever, and she spent many days pondering her dilemma. Then she remembered her Silver Shoes, which had great power and would do almost anything she commanded them. So she used the shoes to create a Magic Chest, and inside it she imprisoned the Shadow. Then the Wicked Witch hid the chest where no one would ever find it – or so she thought. For the Shadow of the Witch is now free and in control of the Emerald City."

The Scarecrow devoted a moment of thought to the words of the Good Witch, and then he said, "It's clear to me that we must locate this Magic Chest."

"But where do we start to look?" asked the Tin Woodman. "The Land of Oz is a large place and this chest could be concealed anywhere."

"I know where it can be found," replied the Witch of the North. "But the journey could prove to be very dangerous."

"Dangerous!" roared the Lion. "Who's afraid of a little danger?"

"Very well, you will find the Magic Chest locked away in a Black Tower that stands at the center of the Great Eastern Forest of Oz. But knowing its location will not make this quest any easier; for the Shadow conjured up this tower with her witch-

craft, and you can be sure it will be filled with traps for the unwary."

"Why didn't she just destroy the chest and be done with it?" asked the Scarecrow.

"She couldn't," replied the little woman. "The Magic Chest was created by the Silver Shoes, and only the Silver Shoes can destroy it. Since the shoes were lost when Dorothy used them to return home, there wasn't any way for the Shadow to accomplish this."

"Then we must go to the Black Tower at once," declared the Scarecrow.

The Good Witch held up a ring made of crystal. "I want you to take this," she told the Scarecrow. "When you find the Magic Chest rub the ring and say the word OZ, and it will instantly transport the three of you to wherever the Shadow may be. But be careful, for the ring will only work once."

The Scarecrow placed the ring on his finger. "I want to thank you for all your help."

"You're welcome," said the Good Witch of the North. "And I wish you all luck." Then she stepped back into the rainbow and disappeared.

And so the three friends set out on their quest to find the Magic Chest.

The Imp

The Emerald City quickly fell to the invaders. The Ozite people were powerless against the savage might of the Hammer-Head soldiers, their flat heads shooting forward on their spring-loaded necks, knocking over anyone who opposed them. Beaten and bruised, the hapless citizens surrendered to their attackers. New laws were immediately posted, and the Ozites were soon reduced to nothing more than slaves. But worst of all, Malvonia had proclaimed herself queen, holding a coronation ceremony on the steps of the Royal Palace.

"This is just the beginning," she had stated publicly, admiring the gold crown placed on her blue head. "Soon all of Oz shall belong to me."

Dark clouds began to gather around the tall spires of the city blocking out the sun, the once-brilliant emeralds that decorated the walls grew dull and lifeless, and a pale mist began to creep over the cobblestone streets. The once-beautiful city was now only a shadow of its former self.

Inside the banquet hall Blugo the Bold was finishing off the remainder of the Dorothy Day celebration cake, when he heard Malvonia scream his name. The Hammer-Head King raced to the throne room as fast as his pudgy legs would carry him, and there he found the Wicked Shadow seated comfortably upon the jewel-studded throne of the Emerald City.

"You wanted me?" he asked.

The Shadow of the Witch looked down at the little king, his chubby face covered with green icing, and she let out a sigh of regret. "Not really," she replied. "But you were the best I could do on such short notice."

"That's not fair," Blugo protested, licking the icing from his lips. "I do my best..."

"Enough!" interrupted Malvonia, sharply. "Has my guest arrived yet?"

"Yes. My soldiers freed him from an enchanted grove in the Winkie Country. He's waiting just outside."

"Then bring him to me immediately!"

Blugo rushed from the room, and when he returned he had an imp beside him. The imp was very nervous and he shook most violently as he approached the throne.

"Are you Imp Etuous?" asked Malvonia.

"I-I-I..." stammered the imp.

"Speak up!" demanded Malvonia.

"I — am," he replied, meekly.

The Imp

"Are you the same Imp Etuous who possesses the magic charm known as the Silver Acorn?" she questioned farther.

"I did – once," he answered.

Malvonia rose to her feet. "You don't have it anymore?"

"No."

"You lost it?" she screamed.

"No!" said Etuous, shrinking away from the Shadow. "It was taken from me."

Malvonia bent over and looked the imp straight in the eyes. "Taken by whom?"

"The Tin Woodman," he blurted out.

"What?!!" shrieked the Shadow, pulling at her blue hair. "I had the Silver Acorn in my grasp and didn't know it?"

"Why would a powerful witch like yourself be so interested in that old thing anyhow?" asked the imp, mystified by all these questions about his former charm. "The Silver Acorn only worked on trees. There are more powerful magic charms to be found in the Land of Oz."

"Fool!" snapped Malvonia, her eyes glowing furiously. "Get out of my sight at once."

Terrified, Etuous fled from the throne room.

"But don't leave the palace," she called after

The Imp

him. "I may have further need of you later."

Once they were alone King Blugo asked, "Why do you want this charm so badly?"

"I'm tired of being just a shadow," replied Malvonia, with a sneer. "But I know how to brew a potion that will make me flesh and blood. All I need is one final ingredient – a magic acorn made of silver."

She reached behind the throne and removed a broomstick. "I must go and search for the Tin Woodman so I can recover the charm. Keep an eye on the Emerald City while I'm gone, Blugo. And if anything is out of place when I return I'll have your flat head."

Then Malvonia put the broomstick between her legs and flew away through an open skylight in the ceiling.

The Silver Acorn

The three companions had been travelling down the Yellow Brick Road for two full days; the Scarecrow led the way, with the Tin Woodman on his right and the Lion pulling up the rear. So far the journey had been pleasant enough – but very uneventful. To keep away the boredom they began to tell stories. The Scarecrow told of how he out-smarted the greedy Crow King, the Lion recounted how he defeated the Great Gray Wolf and finally the Tin Woodman related his encounter with Imp Etuous, showing them the Silver Acorn he had taken away from the wicked little man.

"That's an amazing story, old friend," said the Scarecrow, examining the charm closely with his painted eyes.

"You should get rid of that thing," the Lion told him gruffly. "It can only bring you trouble."

"Well – I think I'll keep it just the same," said the Tin Woodman, placing the magic charm back under his tin cap.

The little company continued along the Yellow Brick Road as it wound its way through the lovely Munchkin countryside. By noon on the third day of the journey they had reached a high hill, and from here they could see the Great Eastern Forest of Oz. The trees stood tall and strong, a thick tangle of blue spruces, elms, cedars, some wispy willows, poplars, hickories and noble oaks. A true sylvan wonderland. But casting a long shadow over all this woodland beauty was a mighty stone tower. It was slender in shape, at least one hundred feet tall, made of solid blocks of black stone and capped by a jagged wooden roof. The tower resembled a monstrous sword that some giant had thrust up from the center of the forest in an attempt to rip a hole in the fabric of the clear noonday sky.

"It looks like we're in for quite a climb," said the Tin Woodman, gazing up at the imposing structure.

Suddenly, the air was filled with a loud cackling. Above them they saw Malvonia hovering over their heads on her broomstick.

"So we meet again, ah, my fine gentlemen," she hissed.

The Scarecrow and the Tin Woodman huddled together out of fear.

Stepping in front of his frightened friends, the

The Silver Acorn

Lion looked up at the Shadow and said, "I'm not afraid of you. Why don't you come down here and face me?"

"I think not," snapped Malvonia. "However, I did bring along an old friend of the Scarecrow. I'm sure he'll gladly accept your challenge."

The Wicked Shadow pointed to a large flock of black crows that were filling up the sky behind her. There were thousands of these birds, and leading them was a large crow with beady eyes.

"That's the greedy Crow King who was after my corn," gasped the Scarecrow.

The Lion's keen eyes watched as the birds grew closer. "I can't protect us against them for long – there are far too many for me to handle alone."

"You're not alone," said the Scarecrow. "I have a better idea, but we have to make it to the forest before those crows reach us."

"You want me to run away from a fight?" growled the Lion.

"We don't have much time to argue about this," said the Scarecrow. "If we're going to get out of this alive you'll just have to trust me."

"I'm willing to give the Scarecrow's plan a chance," said the Tin Woodman.

"All right!" moaned the Lion, shaking his

shaggy head. "Get on my back. I'm faster than either of you and I can carry you to the forest in the blink of an eye."

So the Scarecrow and the Tin Woodman climbed on the Lion's back, grabbing hold of his thick mane for support, and he bore them away.

"Run, fools!" Malvonia thought to herself, as she guided her broom out of the path of the advancing birds. "But the crows are far swifter than you, and they will soon peck you all to pieces. Then I will swoop down and recover the Silver Acorn."

The sky grew dark, as if there had been an eclipse, while thousands of crows swarmed forward like a living cloud, their wings beating so hard they sounded like the rumble of distant thunder. At their head flew the Crow King, his beady eyes filled with hatred for the Scarecrow.

"I promised to get even with you, straw man," the Crow King chuckled wickedly. Then he turned to his troops and squawked, "Faster! They are trying to escape."

The Lion was breathing heavily, but he continued to dash along the Yellow Brick Road without pause. On his back the Scarecrow and the Tin Woodman clung tightly to his shaggy mane as they struggled to keep from falling off. In less than a minute he had carried them to the edge of the forest, and here the Scarecrow called for him to halt.

Turning to the Tin Woodman he said, "Quickly! Give me the Silver Acorn."

Without hesitation the Tin Woodman took the magic charm from under his cap and set it in his friend's outstretched glove.

The Scarecrow held up the Silver Acorn, and in his most commanding voice he said, "Trees of the Great Eastern Forest of Oz! You must all obey me while I hold this charm, and so I order you to keep these wild crows from hurting my friends and me."

A hush fell over the forest, and the air was filled with electricity.

"I sure hope this works," whispered the Tin Woodman.

"Hmph!" said the Lion. "I don't like to rely on magic, so keep your axe handy just in case it's needed."

The crows had finally reached the forest. They shrieked with savage glee as they swooped down between the branches. But their shrieks soon turned to screams as the trees began to move, their wooden limbs wrapping around the black-birds like leafy tentacles, firmly squeezing the life

from their feathered bodies. The dead birds began to rain down on the forest floor – the Crow King being the first to fall. Within minutes most of the flock had been destroyed, and the ones who hadn't entered the forest were flying away in terror.

"We're safe!" shouted the Tin Woodman, overjoyed.

"Not yet," said the Scarecrow. "We still have Malvonia to deal with."

They scanned the sky, but the Shadow was nowhere to be found.

"She's gone," stated the Lion. "This Shadow creature isn't very brave without her servants to back her up."

The Scarecrow returned the Silver Acorn to the Tin Woodman. "We must be very careful from now on," he warned. "Malvonia knows where we are, and with that flying broomstick she can sneak up on us at any time."

"Let her come," snarled the Lion.

The Black Tower

Malvonia had been terribly clever in the construction of her tower. She placed it at the very center of the dense forest, far from any village or road. This insured complete isolation for the dark structure and the Magic Chest it housed.

"If we're to reach the Black Tower we'll have to leave the Yellow Brick Road behind and make our way through the forest," advised the Scarecrow.

The Tin Woodman nodded his head in agreement. "It seems to be the only sound idea. But how will we keep from getting lost in this leafy maze?"

"No problem," announced the Lion, sniffing at the air. "This Black Tower simply reeks of magic. I'll have no trouble picking up its scent and guiding us in the right direction."

"Excellent!" said the Scarecrow. "Let's get started."

The little company went into the forest. They travelled north through the close and gloomy woodland, tramping over tree-covered knolls, around vine-shrouded depressions, and through small, shadowy dells. The going was extremely hard, but just before dusk they reached the base of the Black Tower.

The Black Tower

There was only one entrance to the structure – a small iron door that had been padlocked shut. "This won't be hard to open," said the Tin Woodman, testing the lock. Then he lifted his axe above his head and brought it down on the shackle. Sparks flew in every direction as metal met metal, and the padlock popped open.

"Well done," said the Scarecrow, patting his friend on the back. "Now let's go in and get this Magic Chest," he added, pushing open the iron door.

A huge gray paw reached out from the darkness beyond the door and knocked the Scarecrow off his feet. He landed head first in some shrubbery, as straw flew in every direction. Then a second paw emerged and sent the Tin Woodman spinning into some briar bushes.

"What's this?" roared the Lion.

Out of the tower stepped the Great Gray Wolf, a cruel smile on his long snout, and contempt in his eyes. "Malvonia told me that you would come along eventually," he growled. "All I had to do was wait."

The Lion frowned. "So you're still alive."

"Yes, and we have some unfinished business to attend to."

The Wolf leaped at the Lion; the Lion sprang at the Wolf, and the two clashed in mid-air. A fury of teeth and claws and fur came tumbling to the ground, the two beasts locked in deadly combat.

"There will soon be a new King of the Forest!" snapped the Wolf, his sharp fangs just missing the Lion's left ear.

"Idle boaster!" shouted the Lion, whacking the Wolf aside with a blow of his mighty paw.

Snarling and scratching, the fierce animals struggled back and forth in the dirt, inflicting terrible violence upon each other, and finally rolling out of sight behind a thicket. Dead leaves, branches and tufts of fur flew up into the air, and the very ground seemed to tremble under the weight of their titanic battle.

Then everything stopped, and there was silence.

Slowly the Lion staggered from the thicket. His mane was matted, his body was covered with scratches, but there was a look of triumph in his eyes.

"Are you all right?" asked the Tin Woodman, using his axe to cut himself free from the briar bushes.

"I'm fine," replied the Lion, holding his head up with pride.

"And what about the Great Gray Wolf?" asked the Scarecrow, crawling out of the shrubs.

"He is dead," said the Lion, as he began to enter the Black Tower. "Now let's finish this quest."

Bending over, the Scarecrow gathered up his loose straw from off the ground and stuffed it back inside his jacket, then followed after the Lion.

"Wait!" shouted the Tin Woodman, who was on his hands and knees in front of the briar bushes. "I have lost the Silver Acorn somewhere in this tangle of thorns."

"We don't have time for that now," said the Scarecrow. "But I promise to personally come back here and help you look for it after the Emerald City is liberated."

Reluctantly the Tin Woodman gave up the search and followed after his friend.

They didn't notice Malvonia creeping out of the shadows. She looked over at the entrance to the tower, and a chilling smile crossed her blue lips. Then she began to rummage through the briar bushes, and soon found what she had been searching for – the Silver Acorn. Malvonia grasped it tightly in her right hand, and mounting her broomstick she flew off in the direction of the Emerald City.

The three companions stood at the bottom of an iron staircase that spiraled up through the Black Tower. Cautiously they began to climb, and a half hour later they reached the top of the structure, entering a low, circular room. In the middle of the room sat a glowing blue chest.

"We found it at last," said the Scarecrow, rushing over to the Magic Chest. He turned the brass key that stuck out of the lock and threw open the lid. "Look!" he said, pointing to the bottom of the box. "There is something written here."

"What does it say?" asked the Tin Woodman.

The Scarecrow read the following out loud:

"To keep the Shadow from causing harm,
Hold my lid open and work my charm.

To keep the Shadow held at bay,
This is what you must say:

Zolo, molo, wanka loo,
Ziggy, wiggy, want-a-who,

Goggle, woggle, zoe,
Shadow away you go!

To keep the Shadow out of sight,
Lock me up good and tight."

The Scarecrow was jubilant. "Let's see Malvonia threaten us while we have this."

But the Lion didn't share in his joy. "Something is very wrong here," he said, uneasy. "The Shadow would never have let us get this far without a fight. I don't like it."

"You could be right," said the Scarecrow, thoughtfully. "But I think our first priority should be to get the Magic Chest out of this horrid tower. We can worry about Malvonia later."

"Maybe I can carry it down the steps," said the Tin Woodman, handing his axe to the Scarecrow. He wrapped his metal arms around the glowing box, and with one loud grunt he lifted it off the floor.

Suddenly the tower began to shake.

"What's happening?" shouted the Scarecrow, alarmed.

The huge blocks of stone that made up the Black Tower began to shudder and split away, as dust and small stones poured into the circular room.

"I knew this was all too easy," roared the Lion. "The Magic Chest was a booby trap – rigged in such a way that moving it would cause the tower to collapse. We're going to be buried alive."

The Black Tower swayed to and fro, and then it simply toppled over, crashing to the forest floor.

The Rainbow Army

Night had fallen over the Land of Oz, and most of the inhabitants of the Emerald City were asleep when Malvonia finally returned. She went directly to the kitchen of the Royal Palace, and there she found Imp Etuous by the stove, bent over a black kettle. Inside the kettle bubbled a dark brown potion, which the imp was stirring with a ladle; it smelt so bad he had to hold his nose to keep from inhaling the noxious fumes.

"I have it!" exclaimed the Shadow, holding up the Silver Acorn.

Etuous gasped.

Malvonia walked up to the stove, pushing the imp aside. Her red eyes glared at the muddy mixture, and she smiled. "Ah! It smells wonderful." Then she dropped the Silver Acorn into the kettle.

At first the magic charm just floated there, bobbing up and down on top of the murky surface, but slowly it sank into the potion. Plumes of gray smoke began to rise from the kettle, as did several loud hissing sounds.

The Shadow waved her blue hands over the kettle as she chanted:

"Wigglus, gigglus goo – wagglus, bagglus snoo!"

The Rainbow Army

Her incantation completed, Malvonia stepped back from the stove, staring at the kettle with breathless anticipation.

The potion stopped bubbling, and its color changed from a dark brown to a bright silver. "Finished at last!" she giggled, grabbing the handle of the kettle and lifting it from the stove. "Just one little sip and I will be flesh and blood."

There was a sudden flash of light in a far corner of the kitchen and the Scarecrow, the Tin Woodman and the Lion winked into view. The Tin Woodman was still holding the Magic Chest.

Blinded by the bright flash, Malvonia stumbled backward, slamming into the stove. The impact was so unexpected, and painful, that she lost her grip on the kettle, and it fell to the floor. Her precious potion spilled out before her, seeping through the cracks in the floor boards, where it was lost forever.

"What happened?" asked the Lion, surprised. "Where are we?"

"I used the crystal ring given to me by the Good Witch of the North," replied the Scarecrow. "It seems to have carried us away from the crumbling

Black Tower and into the kitchen of the Royal Palace."

The Shadow looked over at the little company, and her blue face tightened. "Haven't you learned to stay out of my affairs by now?" she shrieked, rushing forward, swinging her broomstick. "I'm going to make a new seat cushion for my throne out of you, Scarecrow. And I'm going to use the Tin Woodman for a hat rack..."

The Lion sprang between his friends and the Shadow, bearing his sharp fangs, and she was stopped cold in her tracks.

"Get out of my way!" screamed Malvonia, bringing her broomstick down hard on the Lion's head.

Angered by this attack, the King of the Forest let out a horrible roar, and it so terrified the Wicked Shadow that she stepped back, shaking before the ire of the enraged beast.

"Now is our chance," said the Scarecrow, "while Malvonia is momentarily distracted."

He threw open the lid of the glowing chest and read the spell written within:

"Zolo, molo, wanka loo,
Ziggy, wiggy, want-a-who!"

Malvonia let out a bone-chilling wail, as her body convulsed violently.

"Goggle, woggle, zoe,
Shadow away you go!"

The Shadow twitched and trembled, as her form began to change. In a few seconds she had become a small blue cloud, and then some unseen force drew the cloud into the Magic Chest. Quickly the Tin Woodman slammed the lid shut, and the Scarecrow locked it up tight with the brass key.

"We did it!" shouted the Tin Woodman, as he set the chest down. "We defeated Malvonia!"

During the excitement they didn't notice the little imp sneaking out of the kitchen. He ran straight to the banquet hall, and there he found King Blugo fast asleep on top of a table. Etuous shook the Hammer-Head King vigorously, and he leaped to his feet. Angry at being so rudely awakened he threatened to smash Etuous to pieces, but the imp stayed well out of reach of his long neck, as he hurriedly told the king what had transpired in the kitchen. Blugo the Bold was outraged, and after calling together twenty of his finest soldiers, he marched off to deal with the intruders.

Back in the kitchen the Lion's ears perked up. "Someone is coming!" he warned.

The Scarecrow, the Tin Woodman and the Lion gathered around the Magic Chest as the Hammer-Head soldiers entered the room.

"You have done me a very great service by getting rid of Malvonia," said the Wicked King, with a smirk. "Now I'm the sole ruler of the Emerald City."

"This isn't working out the way I'd hoped it would," the Scarecrow whispered to his friends.

"And to show my appreciation," continued Blugo, "I will see that you are killed quickly."

Looking around for a means of escape the Lion noticed a pipe that connected the stove to the chimney, and he had an idea. He reached up, his sharp claws extended, and severed the pipe. Instantly the room was filled with thick black smoke, obscuring the Hammer-Heads' vision, and causing them to choke.

"Run!" shouted the Lion.

The three companions fled from the smoke-filled kitchen, rushing down a long hallway, and out a small door which opened onto the cobblestone streets of the Emerald City. The whole city was in darkness, and it was easy for them to disappear into the many winding alleys of the sleeping metropolis. Keeping to sidestreets and back alleys the Lion was able to guide his friends safely around the many Hammer-Head patrols who were searching for them, and soon they arrived at the city gate.

"Open the gate and we'll be safe," said the Lion.

"But the gate is locked!" exclaimed the Scarecrow. "And the Guardian isn't here to open it for us."

"We have a more serious problem coming our way," cried out the Tin Woodman, pointing over his shoulder.

King Blugo was scrambling down the street, his eyes narrowed with anger, the whole Hammmer-Head Army right behind him.

"This looks like the end," moaned the Scarecrow.

Just then the gate swung open on its own.

There stood the Good Witch of the North, a twinkle in her eye and a smile on her lips. Behind her, the Yellow Brick Road was bathed in torchlight, each torch being held by a soldier, who also carried a rather nasty looking spear. A huge army had assembled just outside the walls of the Emerald City. There were Munchkins sporting bright blue uniforms, Winkies in shiny yellow armor, Gillikins wearing purple chainmail, and Quadlings attired in red leather trimmed with gold braids.

When King Blugo saw the massive army, his face turned pale, and he surrendered right there on the spot. "Please have mercy on me," he begged, cowering before the three companions.

Overwhelmed by this strange turn of events, the Scarecrow looked to the Good Witch and asked, "Where did this army come from?"

She walked up to him and placed a dainty hand on his stuffed shoulder. "I once said you had plenty of friends who would help you – and here is the proof. When the good people of Oz heard about your plight they banded together, forming this Rainbow Army, determined to help you regain your throne."

"How very touching," sighed the Tin Woodman. "I think I'm going to cry."

"Don't do it!" ordered the Lion, gravely. "We don't have your oil can with us, and you've been squeaking quite a bit lately."

The Scarecrow stepped outside the city gate and bowed awkwardly to the Rainbow Army. "I never dreamt that I had so many friends," he said,

warmly. "And I want to thank you for all your help."

The soldiers cheered.

Dawn! The warm rays of the morning sun quickly burned away the fog and gloom which hung over the Emerald City, bringing back the brilliant sparkle that made it the crowning jewel of the Land of Oz. Inside the Royal Palace King Blugo and his Hammer-Head soldiers were brought before the Scarecrow, and after agreeing never to invade the Emerald City again – under penalty of losing their flat heads to the chopping block – they were allowed to return to their high hill. As for Imp Etuous, he was captured and carried back to where the Enchanted Trees made him their prisoner once more. And finally, the Magic Chest was entrusted to the Good Witch of the North, and she promised to lock it away where no one would ever find it.

Overjoyed at having their city back, the Ozites threw a huge party for all the people of Oz. It started with a large parade led by the Soldier with the Green Whiskers, who was dressed in his sharpest uniform, his highly polished rifle thrown over his right shoulder. Behind him came many fine marching bands, and the music they made was so grand it inspired the Scarecrow and the Tin Woodman to do a little dance, while the Lion kept the beat with his tail. That night there was a feast, followed by a magnificent fireworks display which lit up the skies above the Emerald City, and a wonderful time was had by all.

Later, after everyone had finally gone home, the Scarecrow retired to his throne room. As he sat alone on the emerald-studded throne he thought about the many kind people who had so selflessly come to his aid, all in the name of friendship, and he smiled. Knowing that he had so many good friends, the Scarecrow was looking forward to the next time he had an adventure in Oz.

The End

Classic Oz Tales
from
Books of Wonder®

The Sea Fairies
by L. Frank Baum
Illustrated by John R. Neill

Dot and Tot of Merryland
by L. Frank Baum
Newly Illustrated by
Donald Abbott

Captain Salt in Oz
by Ruth Plumly Thompson
Illustrated by John R. Neill

The Silver Princess in Oz
by Ruth Plumly Thompson
Illustrated by John R. Neill

The Wonder City of Oz
Written and Illustrated by
John R. Neill

Lucky Bucky in Oz
Written and Illustrated by
John R. Neill

The Magical Mimics in Oz
by Jack Snow
Illustrated by Frank Kramer

Sky Island
by L. Frank Baum
Illustrated by John R. Neill

Merry Go Round in Oz
by Eloise Jarvis McGraw
and Lauren McGraw
Illustrated by Dick Martin

Handy Mandy in Oz
by Ruth Plumly Thompson
Illustrated by John R. Neill

Ozoplaning with the Wizard
by Ruth Plumly Thompson
Illustrated by John R. Neill

The Scalawagons of Oz
Written and Illustrated by
John R. Neill

The Runaway in Oz
by John R. Neill
Illustrated by Eric Shanower

The Shaggy Man of Oz
by Jack Snow
Illustrated by Frank Kramer

If you enjoy the Oz books and want to know more about Oz, you may be interested in **The Royal Club of Oz**. Devoted to America's favorite fairyland, it is a club for everyone who loves the Oz books. For free information, please send a first-class stamp to:

The Royal Club of Oz
P.O. Box 714
New York, New York 10011

Or call toll-free: (800) 207-6968

OZ
from
Emerald City Press™

Exciting Oz Stories
from a New Generation of Authors and Artists

How the Wizard Came to Oz
Written and Illustrated by
Donald Abbott

The Magic Chest of Oz
Written and Illustrated by
Donald Abbott

Father Goose in Oz
Written and Illustrated by
Donald Abbott

The Speckled Rose of Oz
Written and Illustrated by
Donald Abbott

Nome King's Shadow in Oz
by Gilbert M. Sprague
Illustrated by Donald Abbott

The Patchwork Bride of Oz
by Gilbert M. Sprague
Illustrated by Denis McFarling

The Giant Garden of Oz
Written and Illustrated by
Eric Shanower

Masquerade in Oz
Written and Illustrated by
Bill Campbell and Irwin Terry

Queen Ann in Oz
by Karyl Carlson & Eric Gjovaag
Illustrated by William Campbell
and Irwin Terry

The Magic Dishpan of Oz
by Jeff Freedman
Illustrated by Denis McFarling

The Glass Cat of Oz
by David Hulan
Illustrated by George O'Connor

Christmas in Oz
by Robin Hess
Illustrated by Andrew Hess

Adventures Under the Sea!

L. Frank Baum is best known as the author of **The Wonderful Wizard of Oz** (1900) and its thirteen sequels. Baum's other fantasies, though less well known, are equally marvelous. **The Sea Fairies**, first published in 1911, has all the magic excitement and fun for which Baum is so famous.

The Sea Fairies introduces us to Trot and Cap'n Bill, who appear in later Oz books. Their high-spirited adventures in the underwater kingdom of the Mermaids are captured in the numerous illustrations of Oz artist, John R. Neill.

Filled with fanciful characters and a touch of high adventure, **The Sea Fairies** is sure to delight the legion of fans who already love **The Wizard of Oz!**

An Underwater Classic!

Adventures High in the Sky!

L. Frank Baum, creator of Oz — America's favorite wonderland, wrote 14 fabulous tales set in that far-off fairyland. Baum's other fantasies, though less well-known, are equally marvelous. **The Sea Fairies** (1911) and its sequel, **Sky Island** (1912), are packed with the fantasy, humor and fun for which Baum is so justly famous.

Sky Island continues the adventures of young Trot and ol' Cap'n Bill, who also appear in later Oz books. Here their delightful escapades also feature favorite Oz characters Button Bright and Polychrome, the Rainbow's Daughter. As in the Oz books, John R. Neill's numerous pen-and-ink drawings capture all the excitement and joy of this wonderous tale.

Soaring on boundless imagination and filled with breath-taking adventures, **Sky Island** is sure to delight the legions of fans who already love **The Wizard of Oz.**

A High-Flying Classic!

—— OZ TITLES FROM ——
BOOKS of WONDER®
—— CLASSICS ——

The Classic Novels
In Their Original Format

The Wonderful Wizard of Oz
by L. Frank Baum
with 24 full-color plates and
over 130 two-color illustrations
by W.W. Denslow

The Marvelous Land of Oz
by L. Frank Baum
with 16 full-color plates and over
125 black-and-white illustrations
by John R. Neill

Ozma of Oz
by L. Frank Baum
with 42 full-color and
21 two-color illustrations
by John R. Neill

Dorothy and the Wizard in Oz
by L. Frank Baum
with 16 full-color plates and
50 black-and-white illustrations
by John R. Neill

The Road to Oz
by L. Frank Baum
with 126 black-and-white
illustrations on colored papers
by John R. Neill

The Emerald City of Oz
by L. Frank Baum
with 16 full-color plates and
90 black-and-white pictures
by John R. Neill

The Patchwork Girl of Oz
by L. Frank Baum
with 51 full-color and
80 black-and-white illustrations
by John R. Neill

Tik Tok of Oz
by L. Frank Baum
with 12 full-color plates and
80 black-and-white illustrations
by John R. Neill

The Scarecrow of Oz
by L. Frank Baum
with 12 full-color plates and
95 black-and-white illustrations
by John R. Neill
(forthcoming spring 1997)

Little Wizard Stories of Oz
by L. Frank Baum
with 42 full-color and
six black-and-white illustrations
by John R. Neill

Distributed by William Morrow and Company